We Are Patriots

Hope's Revolutionary War Diary

· Book Two ·

by Kristiana Gregory

Scholastic Inc. New York

Valley Forge, Pennsylvania
1777

Thursday, the 2nd of January, 1777
Valley Forge

'Tis a cold, snowy morning and my birthday, too! I am now ten years of age. When I came downstairs for breakfast Mother gave me this new diary. She sewed the pages together herself and made its cover from blue cloth, the same as my dress. Oh, a fine gift it is, for my other diary has no more space in which to write. I shall try to be cheerful but 'tis with a heavy heart that I pick up my pen.

Though 'tis my birthday I must speak of the war. Mother says we received a wonderful present last week when General Washington marched on Trenton. He won the battle yet we still worry. The Redcoats are many. Every day they come closer to our doorsteps and will soon capture Philadelphia. I am too upset to think about it . . . Englishmen taking over our beautiful city!

To be safer, Mother hurried us away from there to the countryside. For two months now we have been staying with Auntie's large family in Valley Forge. We are a day's ride from the city, mayhap seventeen miles. 'Tis far, but methinks not far enough.

Almost noon

I am writing from a stool near the parlor window. Outside are fields of snow. The sky is gray with big snowflakes drifting down. The fences are frosted white. I can see the barn and Uncle at the well, pulling up a pail of water for the animals.

 4

I cannot forget that we are at war with England. Papa has been gone from us more than a year. Where he is and what he is doing is a secret. We know not if he has been hurt or taken prisoner. How we miss him . . . he was away when Mother birthed baby Faith. She is now nearly six months old.

Nor has my brother Ethan seen our baby. To our sorrow he ran away from home last summer. Before Christmas we learned that he was captured by the Redcoats and put into gaol — that is prison. They say he is a spy and want to hang him . . . my poor brother! Fourteen is too young for one's life to end. Mother and I pray every day for him. Friends are working to free him.

Before bed

Thirteen of us are living in Auntie's stone house. Our friends Miss Sarah and Mr. Dean are here as well. They are Quakers who came with us from Philadelphia. Miss Sarah is a young widow whose husband died last year from wounds. That is why she dresses in black. Mr. Dean boarded with us and helps whilst Papa is gone. We are all grateful to be out of the city. How long we will stay here, we know not.

Friday, the 17th of January

Snow again. I love this cozy house, but 'tis crowded and noisy from my many cousins. Four girls and little twin boys. The twins make more trouble than all us girls put together. Up and down the stairs they go, then 'round and 'round the table. They march with loud steps because they pretend to be soldiers. They like the idea of war. Their sisters are not quiet either, how they chit and chat! All the long day. They whisper and giggle and tease. Auntie says another baby will be born this summer. I help her with minding the children and baking. Her oven is like ours at home, built into the bricks, to the side of the fireplace.

Oh, for a quiet moment to myself. I should like time to sew another sampler.

Afternoon

A fortnight has passed since my birthday and I forgot to write of my other gift. 'Twas a brass locket that snaps open like a little book. Inside on the left is an ink drawing of Papa, on the right a lock of his hair. I wear it around my neck on a blue ribbon so I can look at it whenever I please. Every day I wonder when Papa will return to us. Or *if* he will return.

I do not have a lock of Ethan's hair to

remember him by, but I do have something else. Last year he made me a little oak box. I treasure it and think of him every time I touch it. 'Tis long and shallow, with a lid. Inside I keep the five smooth stones Mr. Dean gave me, also my pen. The quill must stay hidden when I am not writing, else the cats — there are five of them — shall chew on the feathers.

Before bed

Now that the house is quiet for the night there is time to write. I am upstairs on my bed. The girls are up here, too, settling under their quilts. Wind is blowing snow against the frosted pane.

Mother scolded me today for rolling my eyes and sighing. 'Tis unkind of me to say this, but I am weary of being here. I want to go home. I miss Polly Adams. She is my best friend, we share all our thoughts and secrets. Home means there shan't be the rabble of so many children and so much work. 'Tis hard being around young ones, hour after hour, day after day. Alas, the wind and ice make it too cold for them to play outdoors.

But they are dear children. As eldest cousin I must be an example and not complain. I pray God will help me be more patient and kind. And thankful. 'Tis far better to be in a crowded house than to be eye to eye with the Redcoats. Now, I must snuff out the candle.

Monday, the 3rd of February

Washday. 'Tis bitter cold out. We boiled a kettle of rice for our noon meal. We drained off the starchy water, then poured it into another pot. This is where we soaked our muslin aprons. Now they are drying with our mobcaps and other wash from rope strung across the room. We starched Uncle's shirts as well.

Too tired to write more.

Next night, before bed

A joyous day!

This morning while I helped Auntie twist dough for pretzels, we heard noise outside. The dog was barking and someone shouted. I hurried to the window to scratch off the ice. A young man was walking slowly up the lane. He was limping. As he came nearer, my heart burst with happiness.

"'Tis Ethan!" I cried.

I know 'twas foolish, but I ran out the door without shawl or shoes. My stockings got wet from snow, yet I cared not. My brother pulled me into his arms.

"Hope Penny," he smiled. "Hast thou been a good lass?"

Of course, said I, laughing. But in my heart I wanted to cry. His face was thin, with dark circles under his eyes. He looked older than fourteen years. And why was he limping?

Mother waited for us in the doorway, holding our baby. Oh the tears, and the laughter. All day we talked. Ethan ate two bowls of chicken stew. I gave him my bread, he was so hungry. I waited until he was done before telling him about the bugs. They were tiny white things crawling around his collar.

Mother wasted no time. Body lice must be killed right away, she said, else they shall be everywhere. After Ethan undressed behind a curtain he scrubbed himself in a hot, soapy bath. Mother boiled his clothes in a kettle.

Whilst they hang to dry overnight, my brother sleeps in one of Uncle's shirts and pair of breeches. His bed is in the barn.

How I thank God my brother is safely home. Alas, my candle is short . . . I shall write on the morrow.

Wednesday, the 5th of February

When Miss Sarah came to breakfast this morning she was not wearing her black dress, but a blue one instead. It matched her eyes and the ribbon on her mobcap. She told us that a year has passed since her husband's death, so she will no longer wear black. Black is for sorrow. Also, black cloth comes from England and we will not purchase goods from our enemy.

Miss Sarah sat down on the bench. I put a bowl of porridge in front of her and one in front of Mr. Dean. As I poured them each a bit of cream I am sure I saw them smile at one another.

Later Mother told me that a Quaker widow might remarry after one year. *Shall there soon be a wedding?*

Next day

This morning whilst I scrubbed pots Ethan told me about gaol. 'Twas crowded with Patriot soldiers, all in irons. Many were dying from wounds and from the cold. There were no privies in the cells so they had to sleep in their own filth. My brother was starved and beaten. A British officer made him take off his shoes and stockings, then he whipped Ethan's feet with a cane. The wounds have not healed so 'tis painful for him to walk.

Before bed last night Mother dressed these

 13

horrible wounds in bandages. She said not a word whilst doing this, but tears ran down her cheeks.

How sorry Ethan is for running away, for causing Mother to cry. He was confused, he said. He thought he wanted to be on the side of King George and be a Tory. When the Redcoats saw that he was just a foolish boy, not a spy, they let him go.

Ethan said that my friend Polly noticed him sitting on our doorstep in Philadelphia. She gave him bread and told him where to find us in Valley Forge. Because he had no money to hire a horse, he walked. It took him four days. Three nights he slept in the snowy woods, without shelter or food. Lice were swarming in his hair and clothes.

Methinks something is not right with Polly's family, the Adamses. She has strong brothers and a father. They have horses, a wagon, mayhap an extra warm coat. *Why did these friends not help my brother travel here?* I am heartsore with worry.

Evening, seven o'clock

I baked an apple cake for Ethan. 'Tis for his missed birthday last December and because he is home. After supper we all gathered around the table to toast him a good year and many more. I wished him to smile, but he just stared at his plate.

"'Twas miserable cold," he said. I fancy he was remembering the gaol. My brother is different now. His eyes are deeper, darker. Methinks he is more a man than a boy. He told us he saw things he cannot speak of yet.

Friday, the 14th of February

This afternoon we stayed by the fire, 'twas so bitter out. Gray light came through the window. Auntie worked at her spinning wheel whilst Mother knitted. I was mending Ethan's shirt.

He sat with us, his sore feet stretched toward the hearth. He told us that when the Redcoats said he could go home they first took off his irons. Then they laughed.

"Run, laddie," they said, pointing guns at him. So Ethan ran. He heard shots and saw mud fly up all around from musket balls striking the ground. The soldiers chased him. Though his feet were bleeding he kept running, just far enough to keep ahead of their shots. Soon the Redcoats grew tired and turned back for their camp. They were playing with him as a cat with a mouse.

Ethan told us the Redcoats look forward to marching into Philadelphia. They believe doing so will end the war. When he said that he wants us to return home, Mother's needles stopped clicking. She looked up.

"Whatever for?" she said.

"We are Patriots, Mother. Papa would want us to protect our house."

For weeks I have so yearned to be home! But now, I am fearful. Yesterday a crier rode horseback through Valley Forge. He warned that the British are coming. 'Tis only a matter of time before they capture Philadelphia. They want our city because 'tis the largest in the Colonies. There could be cannons and bayonets. And if the soldiers were cruel to my brother, how will they treat us? Oh, methinks there is too much danger.

To bed now . . . but how shall I sleep with such worries?

Sunday, the 16th of February

Faith is seven months old today. She crawls about and pulls herself up to stand by the bench. 'Twas a near disaster when she grabbed the tablecloth. Down it came with all that was on it: a cup of white sugar, a large cream pie, some spoons and wooden bowls. Such a clatter! The bowls bounced, then rolled across the floor. The dog leapt for the pie and had it gobbled down in a blink. He was still licking the floor as we swept up the sugar. Before spooning this sugar into our tea we shall need to sift out the dirt!

My cousins are surprised that Faith's middle name is Strawberry. More surprised that Mother let me name her. I told them 'tis because she was born in a strawberry patch on a hot summer night. And because her hair is red.

Faith Strawberry Potter. A fine name,

methinks. She is a plump baby with bright cheeks. To myself I call her my Chubby Strawberry. Oh, did she cry with all that table noise.

Late, near eleven o'clock

This morning after the mess was cleaned up, Mother said she is giving thought to returning home. Ethan talks much about liberty and freedom. Now he wants to join General Washington's army to fight the British. Methinks he is too young for such things! But I look into his eyes and no longer see my carefree brother. He has secrets I know not.

Uncle says that General Washington's army is suffering terribly. His soldiers are leaving him for their homes. He has begged them to stay. He even offered a bonus if they would. Worse, Uncle says that neighbors are joining the

Tories! He said that if you see a red ribbon on a door, it means they are loyal to King George.

Oh, 'tis late . . . I just tucked the girls into their bed and am writing by a short candle. Voices downstairs tell me everyone is still awake. Tea is being served, I can tell from the rattle of cups and saucers. What they are talking about at this late hour, I know not.

The dog is here at my side with one paw on my foot. I like him. When I pet him he wags his tail. I think about Polly and those red ribbons.

Tuesday, the 18th of February
Still in Valley Forge

We leave for Philadelphia on the morrow.

Such a flurry these past hours. Yesterday we did wash, then hung everything around the house to dry. Today we fluffed the feather quilts and put them outside, over the fences to air. I have been sweeping every corner.

Methinks I am too busy to be afraid even though British are camped in New Jersey. 'Tis called the Garden Colony and is the one next to ours. Mr. Dean and Ethan say 'tis safe for us to hurry home. Uncle shall drive us in his wagon.

I had sudden tears when bidding farewell to my cousins.

A few days later
Philadelphia

Home at last. Supper dishes are done, I am writing by the fire. Mother and I are back to sharing her bed while Papa's gone, and Faith has her cradle. Ethan and Mr. Dean sleep in the attic, my old room. Miss Sarah is once again our neighbor. She lives 'round the corner in her

21

fabric shoppe. We share a well out back, and a privy. In summer we share the garden where my Chubby Strawberry was born. Methinks Miss Sarah is lonesome living by herself. She busies herself sewing chair covers and flags for ships.

'Twas a cold journey from Valley Forge into the city. It took one full day. The road was poor, with mud and holes. All the while I was nervous about Redcoats, but we saw none. Only ragged farmers hauling hay and other goods. I looked for red ribbons on houses but saw none.

Our house was as we had left it, boarded up, but what a happy sight. Right away Mother set to opening all the shutters. Mr. Dean took our cart to gather firewood. Ethan went to check on our chickens. We had left them in the care of our good neighbor, Mr. Walker, the wig maker. His tiny shoppe is betwixt our house and Hannie's bakery.

After four months away, our hearth was stone cold, so I ran to Polly Adams's for a light. How glad we both were to see one another! She scooped a long-handled spoon into the ashes of her own hearth. Out came some glowing red coals that she poured into my pail. 'Twas the easiest way to start our fire. As I left, we hugged and promised to see each other again soon.

When our candles were once again lit we could see our rooms. All was well save for some mischief done by mice. They had eaten through a sack of cornmeal we left in the cupboard. I swept their droppings off the windowsills and shelves. There was a foul vapor from this. To sweeten the air Mother boiled lavender leaves with sticks of cinnamon.

In the cellar some of our pumpkins and squash were nibbled. These we tossed into the street for the pigs. They roam the streets like cats. Our three barrels of apples were safe, for we had hammered on their lids.

Before bed

This afternoon Polly came to the door with a basket over her arm. Inside was our good old cat. It had lived with her while we were gone. Now our mice shall stay away or be eaten.

I am happy to be home again, but truth is I miss my little cousins. Now that I think back on their chatter and noise, 'twas not so bad. I regret being snappish.

The same week

Windy and cold now for days.

Mr. Dean has returned to work at the book shoppe. After breakfast this morning he carried in an armload of wood. He was whistling a happy tune. We watched him set the wood down on the hearth, then brush off his hands. I had not seen him this cheerful whilst doing chores, so I asked if he felt well. Just then Miss Sarah came in through our back door. She, too, was smiling.

I am happy to say, our neighbor Miss Sarah shan't be lonesome any more. Mr. Dean has asked her to wed. They marry in three days!

Friday, the 28th of February

'Tis early, not yet dawn. Mother and I are baking Miss Sarah's wedding cake. Flour, sugar, eggs . . . we had to buy these things, as our cupboards were bare. And our hens are not laying, for 'tis been too cold. Mr. Dean sold his sword for shillings, I know not how many. But he gave Mother enough silver coins to get what we need. As the war goes on, our Continental money is worth less and less. It seems that silver and gold have the most value.

On the morrow we shall open our bakery again. Ethan is hanging our sign at this very moment: POTTER'S PIES. Carved into the wood is a picture of a plump golden tart, our specialty. This means I shall rise early before school to help Mother with baking. Every day save Sunday. I forgot to tell that I returned to school last week. Our teacher is new.

Noon

I shall write quickly for Miss Sarah's wedding is in an hour.

The cake has cooled. 'Tis square in shape, frosted white with shavings of chocolate on top. We lay sprigs of evergreen on the plate. There are no flowers, for our garden still lies under a crust of snow.

My dress is clean, and so, too, my cap. Faith looks like a little doll in her knit bonnet! I think 'tis sweet the way her red curls frame her cheeks. Even our brother looks fresh. His white shirt has ruffles at the neck and his breeches tie at his knees with a black satin bow. Then white stockings, buckle shoes, and a tricorn on his head. I say, Ethan has the look of a gentleman. He wears his hair like Mr. Dean, tied back onto his neck.

Must put my pen down . . . 'tis time for our walk to Christ Church.

Before bed

'Twas a quick wedding, just a few of us were there. Polly and Hannie stood with us as the rector read from the Bible. Old Mr. Walker was there, too, leaning on his cane. After the vows we all came here for dinner. Small red potatoes with roasted pig . . . its head shall make a fine stew for the rest of this week.

I want to tell why there was such a small crowd in the church.

Miss Sarah and Mr. Dean are Quakers but, before they even met, they had been read out. This means the Quakers forbid them to step foot into the meeting house and their families shan't speak to them. Why? Quakers have strict rules. They do not believe in taking sides in any war. So when Mr. Dean declared himself a Patriot they shunned him. And Miss Sarah was read out because her papa was against her first marriage, because the man wasn't a Quaker. Methinks shunning is unfair and unkind.

I am sore pleased Sarah and Mr. Dean have each other, and that we are their new family.

Saturday, the 1st of March
Near bedtime

Tonight after supper I carried the dishwater out to our hens. We use no soap when washing pots and bowls, so the water is good for them. In it there are bits of soggy food they can eat. When I closed the door to their little house I looked up at the candle in Miss Sarah's window. I am happy she is no longer alone, that she has a husband to love.

A few moments ago the night watchman passed our house. Through our parlor window I could see his lantern swinging from his hand. He cried out, "A quarter after seven and a-l-l's well!"

I shan't say this aloud, but methinks all is *not* well. How can it be if we are still at war with England?

Monday, the 10th of March

Papa's birthday. I miss him. 'Tis his second year away from us. I baked a small spice cake to honor him. After supper we ate it with our tea.

Tuesday, the 11th of March

I like Teacher this year. His wig is powdered light blue and he wears a blue satin waistcoat. Methinks he is from Boston. He is kind and has not thrashed any of us. Our teacher last year was cruel. He beat my hands with his ruler when I made a mistake in arithmetick. Our schoolroom is two blocks from Market. 'Tis small with a fireplace and benches. A window facing the street makes me want to look outside.

Today, for some reason, Polly sat next to me but spoke not! After school she hurried home without me. I thought mayhap I had done something to offend, so I went to her house. She peered out her door to say she could not visit. Her father, Mr. Adams, shouted something from inside, I heard not what. Then Polly closed the door.

Tears stung my eyes. I have been kind to her. We have had no spats. Oh, what could the matter be? I am heartsore about this.

Friday, the 14th of March

I am writing from the attic, from my stool by the window. 'Tis my own room again! When Mr. Dean wed Miss Sarah, he moved his few things from here into her house. And Ethan prefers to sleep down by the fire. This way he can reach our musket if there is trouble.

'Tis small up here. My bed is under the low slant of the roof, near the warm chimney. At night I carry up a hot brick wrapped in cloth, to put under my blanket. It heats my bed nicely — so does our good old cat.

When the candle is down I like to look out the window. Our neighborhood is dark save for the tall street lamp 'round the corner. Every night the lamplighter brings his ladder to climb up. He fills the lamp with whale oil, then lights it with a candle from his own lantern. If the moon is full he stays home, for the streets are bright enough. Doing so saves oil.

I love my room. During the day I can look out over the rooftops, toward the harbor. If a ship sails upriver from the ocean, I shall see her tall masts and sails. I have not lost hope that Papa may be on one of those ships.

Thursday, the 20th of March

This morning I went to market to buy meat for Mother's pot. We had heard the bell ring from one of the sheds there. This means someone has arrived from the countryside with fresh provisions. I noticed Polly's mother in the crowd near us.

"Halloo, Mrs. Adams," I said. When she looked away I though mayhap she knew not who had spoken. I greeted her again and smiled. This time she gave me a cold, hard stare. Then something happened that I shall ne'er forget.

Under her breath she said, "Rebel."

A chill ran through me. Only someone loyal to King George would call me Rebel. Such was the sick feeling in my stomach that I clutched the front of my apron and ran home.

Before bed

'Tis near nine o'clock and all is not well.

Over tea Miss Sarah told us that Polly's

family has turned coat. That is, they side with the Redcoats. They are Tories . . . my best friend! Does this mean she is my enemy? I am sick about this. Mother is angry.

"Traitors!" she cried. She said this with such fury tears came to her eyes. "Thy brother near died from the Redcoats' cruelty. . . ." She said more but I shan't write it.

Sunday, the 23rd of March

Church. 'Twas like ice inside though my feet rested on a coal heater. The rector said the Colonies are full of Tories, some may even be our neighbors. I bowed my head at his words. To myself I thought, *Yea, even dear friends can be Loyalists.* Oh, I am heartsore. I prayed for Polly . . . mayhap we need not be enemies. The singing of hymns comforted me.

Faith has a cold. She kept Mother awake

all night with her coughing. Methinks I, too, am ill.

Monday, the 7th of April

Have not written for a fortnight. Fourteen nights I slept as if dead, such was my fever. Mother and Ethan, too. Our good neighbors came to tend our fire and soup pot. Miss Sarah cared for Faith as if she were her own babe. To cheer me, Mr. Walker brought a pretty yellow ribbon from his wig shoppe, for my hair. He is a dear old man.

Every day Hannie came with fresh rolls from her bakery. Today is the first morning Mother is able to be up at the hearth. Our oven is warm, dough on the table is rising. I shall help her now.

Why did Polly not call on me . . . was she also ill? Or does war separate best friends?

Thursday, the 10th of April

This morning I tore paper from this journal for a letter to Polly. 'Twas brief: *Dear friend, I miss you. Are you well? Please come for tea. Love, Hope.*

Then I wrapped a warm apple tart into a cloth and hurried to Polly's house. Her little brother answered my knock. Through the open door I saw the hearth ablaze and Polly sitting in a rocker. When I set my gift in her lap, she looked at me with sad eyes. "You must leave quickly, Hope," she said.

'Tis nightfall. I look through my window to the street below. At Polly's house a candle casts yellow light out across the cobblestones. If her mother forbids her to visit me, mayhap we can meet in secret.

Saturday, the 12th of April

'Tis nearly time for supper so I must move my pen quickly . . . oh, the news we have treasured today!

When I was at market this morning, a farmer greeted me with a lift of his hat. "Good day, miss," he said. "Regards to your mother." From his sleeve he pulled out a folded piece of paper, which he dropped into my basket.

"Your name, sir?" I asked. But he turned and walked away.

His silence made me fearful so I hurried home. Mother unfolded the paper and leaned toward the fire to read in its light. When she clapped her hand over her mouth and began to cry, I worried 'twas terrible news. But suddenly she was laughing and holding her arms up to praise God.

Papa is coming. We have not set eyes on

him since four months and one year. Oh joy!
Before the next rooster crows my father shall
once again be under our roof.

After supper

I have washed all the cups and bowls and
helped Mother bake a pan of shortcake. Ethan
has brought in wood to last through the night.
It might be a late one, for the note said Papa
shall arrive in the wee hours. A tall candle sits
on the windowsill so Papa shall be able to find
his way. I am stirred beyond words.

Half past three in the morning

None of us has gone to bed yet. I am up in
my room looking out the window. 'Tis still
dark, the streets are wet with rain. In a few

hours the lamplighter shall come by with his ladder to snuff out the street lamp.

Joy of joys, my father is home. The kitchen is aclatter with breakfast starting. I smell bacon and fried potatoes. But news first. . . .

Just after midnight we heard footsteps then the latch rattled and our door opened. I jumped up from my bench. Truth be told, I had been dozing, my head on the table. I ran into Papa's arms, Mother reached him the next moment. Ethan cried, "Father!"

We made Papa sit in a chair close to the hearth, for he was shivering with cold. He kept looking in the cradle at Faith. 'Twas the first time he had set eyes on her. When the firelight glowed upon Papa's face I saw how lean and weary he was. First Ethan, now my father. This war is a suffering thing.

Mother handed him a bowl of soup. Only

then did we see that his left hand was missing! A bandaged stump moved out from the sleeve of his coat. I was horror-struck. I thought mayhap Mother would faint, yet she stood brave.

"Thomas, what happened to thy hand?" she asked.

A cough shook his thin shoulders. "A cutlass, my dear, from one cruel stroke by a Redcoat." Then Papa told us his story. We are not to speak of it to a living soul, but I shall write it here. 'Twill be safe on these pages. I hide this diary inside the feathers of my bed. It makes a little lump when I sleep, but bothers me not.

Later

Out the window I can see Miss Sarah and Mr. Dean walking in the rain toward our door. They come for tea and to welcome my father.

To finish Papa's story . . . some years ago

colonists grew angry with King George. His taxes and laws were harsh. To protest these laws, a group of men got together and called themselves the Sons of Liberty. They made secret raids to show that the spirit of resistance was growing. One time they dressed up like native Indians and snuck aboard ships in the Boston harbor. These ships were from England, full of English tea. The tax on this tea was so high that the Sons of Liberty dumped it overboard. Just to show the king that Americans were tired of his rules. This was four years ago, before Papa sailed to Boston to join them.

They made other attacks, some with no bloodshed, some with. Ethan asked our father if he had ever killed a man. Papa looked into the fire, then looked at the stump of his hand. He nodded.

The secret that we must keep in our family is that Papa was with the Sons of Liberty. The

British are coming closer and may capture our city. If they learn that Papa killed one of them, they shall hang him. Though he is home, I still wear my locket with the drawing of him and the lock of his hair. I love it so.

Saturday, the 26th of April

Sunny today, but a fierce wind. I walked to the paper shoppe to deliver a basket of meat pies. On the way home I stopped in front of Mr. Walker's shoppe. He was in the window, putting a new wig onto a dummy's head. With a smile he waved me in. He asked if I would go to market for him, as his legs ached from the cold. Gladly, said I.

He put a shilling into my palm. At market I bought cloves, ground cinnamon, a three-pound sack of flour, and other victuals. When

I returned with my full basket, he bade me stay for tea. He is our friend so I set his small kettle over the fire and put two cups with saucers onto his table.

Whilst our water heated he mixed the spices and flour in a bowl. This he rubbed into the hair of a wig that had been brought to him for cleaning. After he combed out the grease and dirt he plaited a pigtail then tied it at the top and bottom with black bows. Quite fancy and sweet smelling.

Next he filled his powder puffer. 'Tis like a box with a hole that lets you squeeze out the powder. It floated onto the hair like snow. And floated all about the walls, the table and floor . . . such a mess! I swept for Mr. Walker, then tidied his cupboards. I minded not that the powder was also in our cups. Next time I shall bring him a plate of johnnycake so he shall have a little something to eat with his tea.

Methinks the wig still had fleas, but I said naught. It belongs to the book shoppe owner. He shall pick it up on the morrow.

Wednesday, the 30th of April

Color has returned to Papa's cheeks. He looks rested and well. Methinks his stump pains him, yet he complains not. Each morning he rises before dawn to bake our bread and pies. Mother and I knead the dough for him when his hand tires. He uses our peel to take loaves from the oven. 'Tis like a flat shovel with a long wooden handle.

For filling, I bring little red apples from the cellar. 'Tis work to cut out the seeds. Whilst the apples simmer in a pot I stir in sugar, cinnamon, and nutmeg, sometimes butter. This we also do with dried apricots and peaches.

Papa listens for the town crier, to hear news of the war. He fears Redcoats shall soon march in our streets. We all fear this yet we must carry on. Ethan spends his days with the ship builder, to learn his trade.

Next day

When Faith crawls along the floor to my father he lifts her to his knee. "Hello, little daughter," he says. She calls him "Baba," then they both laugh.

'Tis a sight that brings Mother to smile.

In the evenings Mr. Dean and Papa talk about the war. They say the difference between Patriots and our enemies is that we fight for liberty. For an ideal. The Redcoats are fighting for money and land. That means if they win this war, all the good things in America shall belong to England. King George hired German soldiers to fight against us. They, too, are in this war for money. They are called Hessians and are most mean.

Tuesday, the 6th of May

No word from Polly. This afternoon when I saw her brother flying a kite along the wharf I whispered a secret to him, to tell Polly. He promised he would if I gave him a berry tart. He is a sweet lad, yet I know not if I can trust him.

Next day

After baking this morning I left early for school. 'Twas cold outside, with ice in the gutters, but my cloak and cap kept the wind's chill from me. Though the stepping-stones were slippery I hurried toward the harbor where there is a dressmaker's shoppe. She is a friend of Miss Sarah's. A light was in the window. When I opened the door there was a tinkling of a little bell from its latch. My heart leapt with happiness. Polly was standing by the fire, waiting for me!

I shall reward her brother with another berry tart.

Polly cried when I told her how I have missed her.

"'Tis Mama and Papa," she wept. "They are loyal to King George and forbid me to see you. I am forbidden to speak to you in school."

I put my arms around her. "Oh, Polly," I said, "thou art my dearest friend. Please do not hate me because of the war."

We spoke for just five minutes, then bade

farewell. We hurried to school by different paths.

Wednesday, the 14th of May

This morning after breakfast my Chubby Strawberry tried to walk! She is just ten months old, yet she is strong and has her own mind. Mother says 'tis her red hair that makes her fiery, but methinks 'tis just the way she is. Faith pulls herself up on Papa's chair then hangs on whilst she steps around. Today when she let go, she took two steps, wobbled a bit, then fell. Her hands and smock are always dirty.

Today in school Polly and I sat on the same bench. We worry someone will tell her parents if we speak to each other so we keep our eyes on Teacher. He gives us our lessons, we answer in turn. 'Tis hard for me not to whisper to her!

During Latin one of the littlest boys spilled his ink jug. Its puddle spread along the floor toward Teacher's fine leather shoes. I dared not look at Polly. Surely we would have laughed. And our giggles would give away our friendship.

So this is what we do. Every third day we meet before supper at the dressmaker's shoppe. 'Tis our secret, only the lady knows. She smiles when we come through her door, then she busies herself without a word. Polly and I are full of chat for ten minutes, then we thank the lady and quickly return to our homes.

I am happy to see my friend again. But what shall happen if our mothers learn that we visit each other?

Friday, the 16th of May

Spring is near! Dogwoods are blooming and some tiny flowers appeared in the churchyard.

I can walk to market without my cloak, just a shawl and cap. I feel like skipping and waving my arms. Hannie's little children draw on the ground with charcoal. They are playing hopscotch in the sunshine.

Papa met secretly with some of his friends late last night. I listened from the attic, for there are cracks in my floor and I can see down to the parlor. They were upset. The British have near 20,000 soldiers ready to march into our city when they break winter camp. Our General Washington is camped in Morristown, but our soldiers are ragged. They have not enough food or clothes. Many are barefoot.

Papa fears we are no match for the Redcoats for they greatly outnumber us. He said we could lose the war in the next few months.

Thursday, the 22nd of May

A lady came to our door this afternoon to buy meat pies for her family. She paid with paper money. After she left Papa let out a happy yell. He showed me the two-dollar note. 'Twas square and fit in my palm. And 'twas newly printed with the words "United States of North America." No longer will our money say "United Colonies" because no longer do we belong to England.

"Day by day we are declaring our independence," Papa said. "No matter what King George and his generals say. If only our brave lads continue to fight."

Friday, the 30th of May

Visitors! My Uncle Ben Potter is here from Trenton with his wife. She is fifteen years old.

Their manner of speech is British, for they sailed here not long ago. 'Tis true that many of us speak the King's English, so do Mother and Papa. All of us were born in England, save Faith.

Uncle Ben said he watched the Battle of Trenton from his upstairs window, day after Christmas. When the smoke cleared, he saw our soldiers fighting the Hessians.

"Our men looked starved and cold," Uncle said. "Yet they were brave and fought hard. 'Twas such a sight. They may have saved us from untold cruelties."

Uncle Ben and his wife, Rachel, are bedding tonight in front of our fire. They shall stay another day before hiring a wagon for Valley Forge. Until the war is over they want to live safely with our Potter cousins, for Aunt Rachel is with child. I told them about the good old dog, the five cats, and all the busy little children. Mr. Walker is giving them a letter for his son, a carpenter, who also lives in Valley Forge.

I wonder if Auntie's new baby is born yet.

Saturday, the 31st of May

The days feel warmer, no more ice in the streets. I waited this morning at the dressmaker's shoppe, yet Polly did not come. We last parted with a friendly kiss, so I know 'tis not a spat that keeps us apart. When Mother saw my sad face, she bent down to kiss my cheek. I feared telling her my worries about Polly.

The cat sits on my lap as I write this. Her purring comforts me.

Thursday, the 12th of June

'Tis hot. I busy myself with chores and helping Papa bake. We have taken the cloth off our table until Faith can walk without grabbing things. Twice this week she pulled it off with all our supper dishes as she tried to move along the bench. The mess and noise of things falling . . . oh, the wail she let out!

The Redcoats are marching toward New Brunswick. Those horrid soldiers are burning down every Patriot house and barn along the way. The countryside is in flames! If they capture our city, will they burn our home, too? Teacher told us about the red ribbons Tories hang by their doors. This way their houses will be spared.

Papa said we shall never hang a red ribbon. Never.

Saturday, the 14th of June

Today is a new holiday. The Continental Congress says we now have an official flag. It has thirteen red and white stripes. In the top corner there are thirteen stars in a blue square. This is to honor our thirteen states. The British flag has the same colors.

Papa said 'tis another sign of our independence, having our own flag. Miss Sarah is sewing some to sell in her shoppe. Now our army shall march with the Stars and Stripes.

Once again Polly did not come to the dressmaker's. It has been a fortnight — fourteen days! — since we last saw each other. I worry she may be ill. Or her parents learned our secret.

Because 'tis summer, the lamplighter comes later, near nine o'clock. Last full moon he stayed home for six days. The sky was bright as the moon waxed, then waned.

The heat makes my upstairs room miserable. Now I sleep in the cellar with Faith. Mother made us cozy soft beds on the stone floor, where 'tis cooler.

After supper

Today Miss Sarah gave me a small flag for my very own. 'Tis the size of a bread plate. I was sore happy as I stood on my toes to kiss her.

Our neighbor across the street died this evening. Her dress caught fire whilst she was cooking supper. She leaves five little children. Methinks her poor husband shall be quick to find a new wife.

Monday, the 30th of June

Fireflies were in our garden at sunset. Their tiny lights flicked here and there. Faith thinks they are fairies. Our cat jumped in the air and caught one. Faith cried to see that when lying in the dirt 'twas just a bug, not a pretty fairy.

Mother and Papa sat next to us on a bench,

for 'twas cooler here than in the house. Miss Sarah and Mr. Dean spread a blanket on the ground to visit with us. We stayed thus until mosquitoes swarmed thick around our faces.

I go to bed with a heavy heart. Papa, Ethan, and Mr. Dean spoke of becoming soldiers for General Washington.

"We are Patriots," they told us.

This I know, but must my father and brother be gone from us again?

Before bed

This morning I walked to the dressmaker's shoppe. The lady handed me a letter sealed with wax. I opened it and leaned toward the window's light. This is what it said: *Dear Hope, Brother told Papa about our visits. He said if I am a friend with a Rebel he shall shave my head bald. I grieve that we are forbidden to see each other.*

But Papa said naught about writing *to a Patriot. I* wait written *word from you and I do remain thy loyal friend. Love, Polly.*

My heart swelled with hope . . . we shall stay friends by pen!

Next day, noon

After breakfast I rolled out dough for cookies. They are dark with molasses and ginger. Before sliding them into the oven on the peel, I flattened each one with a fork to make lines. Then I pinched sugar from the bowl and sprinkled the tops. Methinks they look less plain this way. After they had cooled I packed them in a clean cloth for the dressmaker. When I arrived at her shoppe with my letter for Polly, she smiled and put her finger to her lips. Our secret is safe with her.

Friday, the 4th of July

The boom of cannons woke us early. My heart raced, thinking war was in our streets. But 'twas just the start of a happy day — the first birthday of our new country. The bell in the Statehouse rang and rang from its tall steeple. Methinks many fingers were busy sewing throughout the city, for our flags were everywhere. All sizes.

People gathered on our corner to hear Hannie's husband read the Declaration of Independence. He stood in his baker's apron, a tricorn on his head to shade his face from the hot sun. His sleeves were rolled above his elbows. Like many bakers, the hair on his arms is burned off.

I looked down the street toward Polly's house. For shame . . . a Stars and Stripes was hanging above their window . . . a Patriot flag in a Tory home! Polly wrote in her last letter to me that her parents are pretending. They fear that neighbors might tar and feather them if they learn of their loyalty to King George.

Mother and Papa know the Adamses are traitors yet they keep their anger to themselves.

Before bed

'Tis late now. The lamplighter just lit our street. His ladder rattles against the post when he climbs up, then down.

Ethan fell asleep on the floor under our table. Papa said he did too much celebrating. Methinks 'twas too much grog, for I can smell the rum from here.

My poor cat hid under my bed from the noise.

Wednesday, the 16th of July

Chubby Strawberry is one year old today. She walks on her own with just a little wobble. I sewed her a mobcap with a blue ribbon like mine. We look like sisters, Papa says. When he calls us his darling girls I feel a new love for him. How I missed him all those months.

After my quiet visit to the dressmaker's shoppe, I tucked Polly's letter inside my sleeve and walked home along Dock Creek. What a stink! The heat makes everything smell bad. Methinks the water is full of rotting food and waste.

'Tis been too hot to write and there is no time. Every day there is baking and chores, then I must go to market to sell tarts. Later I take Faith out for a stroll, but 'tis work keeping her from running into the street. A horse reared up yesterday and near kicked her, but I grabbed her away in time. After supper dishes I just want to sit in the garden. And I would sleep there save for mosquitoes. At night Papa pulls the shutters closed, then locks our doors for safety. 'Tis so hot I lie on my bed with no cover, even in the cellar. Methinks not one of us sleeps much.

Before bed

A letter from Auntie. She birthed a baby boy in June . . . but he lived only three days. I know not if they gave him a name.

Thursday, the 31st of July

Teacher has been ill so there has been no school. Methinks he has the pox, poor man! I want to keep learning so I read the *Evening Post* and the Bible. To keep my penmanship neat, I write verses on a slate and write in this diary. Arithmetick I practice at market. Mother says 'tis good to know these things, but a girl must also sew and cook and have a kind heart.

She gave me a proverb to stitch onto my new sampler: *Let not mercy and Truth forsake thee: bind Them about thy neck; write Them upon the tablet of thine heart.* I fancy using blue thread with a red border. Mayhap I shall sew in thirteen white stars.

Criers rode through the streets with frightful news: The British fleet is anchored at the mouth of Delaware Bay! The ships could sail right to Philadelphia . . . all of us fear our city shall soon be invaded.

Papa has only one hand yet he says he can fight the Redcoats like any man. Ethan is begging to go as well. They and Mr. Dean want to join the Continentals right away. This worries me sick. I cannot bear the thought of Papa leaving again, nor my brother.

Wednesday, the 13th of August

This morning whilst Mother and I baked the pies she told me something dreadful. Papa is a wanted man, she said. Wanted by the British. If our city is soon to be captured, Papa must hide, else they shall put him in prison. But my father is brave. He refuses to hide. He says the honorable thing for him is to help General Washington; 'tis best to face the enemy as a soldier ready to fight.

Papa is giving careful thought to when he should bid us farewell. Ethan must stay to protect us, he said. My brother is restless. He wants to fight the English, but he also wants to obey Papa. I pray he does not run away again. Mother and I need him.

Mr. Dean hurried from the book shoppe with news. British warships are off the coast of Maryland, just thirty miles below the Delaware capes. But they are sailing south, away from us! He thinks they are trying to fool General Washington. There is much confusion and worry.

Later

Miss Sarah came for tea this afternoon. She was rosy from the heat, but very happy. She is with child! I am curious about the thoughts in my head . . . one minute I feel terror about the Redcoats, the next I am excited about a baby coming. Mother said this is life. For every sorrow there is joy, for every worry there is hope. No matter what the war brings, we shall see a new baby next spring. I pray it does not die after three days, but lives a full life.

Next week sometime

It rained for two days. We were much relieved by the cooler air and the streets washed clean. Now 'tis hot once more.

Still no school. Oh, I am lonesome for Polly. Letters are good, but I miss seeing her. Her voice always cheers me. When summer was too hot we waded together near the harbor. But not this year.

Sunday, the 24th of August

Much has happened. As the Redcoats come closer Papa has prepared us for his leaving. We now have two muskets, and Ethan knows how to melt lead into bullets. The shelves in the cellar are full: there are sacks of flour, sugar, salt, and dried beef, and jugs of fruit. Our apple

 66

barrels are near empty. We shall fill them at harvest when farmers come to market.

Mother wept not when Papa bade farewell with Mr. Dean. They left in the wee hours some days ago, to serve with General Wayne's men. Miss Sarah shall stay with us, for if soldiers learn she lives alone they might harm her. Ethan latched her shutters closed and put padlocks on each door. A sign in her shoppe window says NOT OPEN.

After supper I shall write of the parade. Heat hangs heavy in the house. When our baking is done in the morning we let the fire go low. Thus, we are not cooking as much. Tonight we are eating from our garden: lettuce with oil and salt, also melons and berries.

Before bed

There was great excitement when General Washington led his army through our city. Riding horseback beside him was Major General Lafayette. 'Twas a handsome sight, these officers in trim blue coats, white breeches, and boots. When Lafayette passed our corner he gave me the compliment of his hat . . . his face is smooth and he looks as young as my brother! Teacher had told us that he is just twenty years old, but very wise. He sailed from France to South Carolina to help our army. He is a French noble, a Marquis.

"The French hate the British," Teacher told us. "So they share our dream of liberty. Mayhap they shall help us win the war."

The Continentals are on the way to fight the British, to defend Philadelphia. People in the crowd said the army would go to the

Brandywine Creek. 'Tis not far from our beloved city.

We stood on a walkway to watch, waving the Stars and Stripes. Even Faith held a little flag. The soldiers wore no uniforms, but were dressed in their everyday clothes. I could see farmers, shoemakers, tailors, and clerks. Many carried muskets over their shoulders, some had bayonets, others wore swords at their waists. In front was a row of young boys playing drums and fifes.

'Twas thrilling to hear the music and see our soldiers' proud steps. Though they passed quickly we did catch sight of Papa and Mr. Dean. Mother stood brave in her best bonnet and clean apron, but I saw tears in her eyes.

I fear what lies ahead.

Friday, the 5th of September

'Tis cooler this week. The air smells of wood smoke and apples baking. No word from Papa.

I'm upstairs, writing by a new candle. The night watchman just cried out, "Quarter past eight and a-l-l-s well!" I pray 'tis true.

Ethan often climbs the stairs to look out my window. He watches for signs of trouble. I am sorry for him. He wants to march with Papa yet his duty is to us. There are boys much younger than he, drumming or taking care of horses for General Washington.

Polly and I trade letters every three days. Methinks our secret is safe with the dressmaker. After visiting her shoppe I am careful to keep Polly's note in my sleeve. Then I hide it in my bed, under the blanket. The last thing I do before blowing out my candle is read what she has written.

She is well, but she is as lonesome as I.

Wednesday, the 10th of September

The city is astir. We fear the Redcoats shall burn our homes and churches if they defeat our army. Ethan is helping other Patriots carry books from the library out to wagons. These and court papers shall be taken to safety, some place far from Philadelphia. Bells from churches and meeting houses are also being taken away. This way the British cannot find them. They would just melt them down for more cannon balls and bullets.

Ethan says if he cannot carry a gun for the Continentals, he at least can help save the bells and our important records.

 71

Next day, ten o'clock in the evening

My head hurts from worry. There is so much happening, I yearn for Polly to be at my side. Her last letter said she shares my distress. If we could just visit face-to-face, our chat would calm us down.

This afternoon we heard the low rumble of cannons, as if 'twas thunder far off. Criers rode through the streets shouting news that there is a battle at the Brandywine. 'Tis miles from here, yet still we could hear. Our army is fighting the Redcoats. We believe Papa and Mr. Dean are there. I pray with all my heart they have not been wounded.

I am too heartsore to sleep.

Monday, the 15th of September

No word from Papa. Mother said we can do naught but pray and trust God.

Miss Sarah sleeps on a daybed in the parlor. She is cheerful and busy, always ready to help. She has already lost one husband to the war, I pray she shall not lose Mr. Dean as well. Faith climbs on her lap every time she sits in our rocker to do needlework.

When I worry I read the Psalms. Also I take out a treasure from my little oak chest. 'Tis a tiny sack with five smooth stones inside. I have cherished these since the day Mr. Dean, who found them in a creek last year, gave them to me. They remind us to be brave. They are from the old story about a shepherd boy named David and a giant named Goliath. David took five stones from a stream. He trusted God to help him fight the giant. And with just one stone in his sling he was able to kill his enemy.

Mr. Dean said that if David could face Goliath, we can stand up to the mighty king of England. "For nothing is impossible with God," he told me.

Our army fought hard at Brandywine Creek, now 'tis on the outskirts of Philadelphia, ready to do battle again.

Friday, the 19th of September

At one o'clock this morning we woke to someone pounding on our door and shouting: "The Redcoats are coming!"

Ethan lit a candle. He and I stepped outside. The streets were aclatter with wagons and carts piled high with furniture and boxes. People were fleeing the city before our eyes. We turned to Mother who stood in the doorway, drawing her shawl about her. In the candlelight her face looked like stone.

"We are staying," she said. "This is our home."

Three days later

I am trying to keep my mind as busy as my hands, but oh, 'tis hard. Yesterday there was a cruel battle not far from here, at Paoli Tavern. So many of our soldiers were killed. The British made a surprise attack whilst they sat around campfires. We know not the fate of Papa or Mr. Dean. I am fearful because 'twas General Wayne's army men who were attacked.

I want to panic, but 'tis my job to stay cheerful for Faith. Mother and Miss Sarah are busy keeping our bakery open. Ethan works at the harbor and watches the river. At the first sign of British ships, he shall run and tell us.

We worry that General Washington's ragged army cannot stop the British from marching into our city. They want Philadelphia for their own because 'tis America's capital, the largest city in the Colonies.

Evening, before bed

What a sight yesterday. Congressmen who were in town heard of the attack at Paoli. Most of them are older gentlemen. Fearing for their lives they fled the city in coaches, for the safety of York. This town is west from here, many days away, across the wide Susquehanna River.

Tuesday, the 23rd of September

As I ready for bed I must tell of the great bell. This is the bell that rang last year after the Declaration of Independence was read from the Statehouse steps. I remember its beautiful tone. Today, 'twas taken down from its steeple and loaded onto a wagon. Hannie's children and I gathered around to see. Carved into the bell are the words, PROCLAIM LIBERTY THRO' ALL THE LAND TO ALL THE INHABITANTS THEREOF — LEVITICUS XXV:X. Methinks those are beautiful words. I am glad the bell is being taken to safety. Someone said it shall be hidden in Allentown, a town to the north.

Next day

We were surprised this morning by a visitor. He handed me a letter, then rushed away when we put a coin in his palm. Ethan and I read it over Mother's shoulder . . . 'twas from Papa!

> *My dear family: Mr. Dean and I are well, serving as you know under the able General Wayne. We saw fierce fighting at Brandywine and Paoli Tavern and, God be praised, we suffered no wounds. But the losses to our Continentals have been great . . . hundreds of Patriots lie buried in the fields. Many dozens of our men, some of them our neighbors, were captured. I fear there are not enough of us left to stop the enemy from taking Philadelphia. Thus, dear ones, I beg you to be brave. I shall visit you as soon as I am able. Your loving Papa.*

Thursday, the 25th of September

Criers shouted that General Howe has split his army in two . . . the Redcoats are just miles from here, about to enter Philadelphia! General Howe sent orders to all of us citizens. He said we are to remain in our homes. If we do so, his soldiers shall not harm us. My heart beats fast to think of the enemy coming. I fear they shall set fire to our house and that they shall hurt us, too.

It rained hard for several hours. 'Tis cold out but our hearth is warm. Faith is walking and talking. She thinks we are planning a party with all our cooking and cleaning. She knows not that 'tis nervousness and fear that keep us busy.

As I write from upstairs I can see out my window. A mean thing is happening. People loyal to King George are roaming the streets, looking for Patriots. They are dragging them out of their houses. Word is that they are putting them in the gaol on Walnut Street.

When we heard of this, we hid Ethan inside Miss Sarah's shoppe. Then we padlocked the door again so it would look as if the house was empty. No sooner had we done so than Mother and I answered a pounding at our own door. Three men we had never seen before ordered us to tell them if we serve King George. Mother answered: "Please leave us alone. We are just women and a baby with no man under this roof."

'Twas the truth. She bade them search if they willed, but they left. Mother stood by the fire to get warm. Her hands were shaking. When we were sure the men had gone, we unlocked Ethan from his hiding place.

Next day, after supper

The English are in our house! They have captured our city!

I am writing by a short candle in Mother's room; Faith sleeps near me on her trundle. The door is ajar so I can see into the parlor. Six Redcoats are sitting in front of our fire! They are wearing tall black boots with white breeches; their hats they have laid on the table. Six bayonets lean against the wall. They took our muskets.

I write this quickly, before Mother calls me to help. She and Miss Sarah are serving them bread with bowls of soup. Ethan is putting on more wood. I am too upset to write more.

Later, near nine o'clock

Mother and Miss Sarah are sharing a bed; I shall sleep in the trundle with Faith. Our door is closed yet we can still hear the Redcoats in the next room laughing. When I last saw them some were drinking ale with their feet propped against our hearth. Others were playing cards. Methinks they plan to bed upstairs in the attic . . . my little room! It shall ne'er be the same.

Saturday, the 27th of September

Friday was a sad day for us.

The British General Howe led his army through our streets in their scarlet uniforms. I hated the sight of them. General Howe passed close enough that I could see he is missing some teeth. He looked well fed, as if the buttons might pop from his coat. There was gold lace on his sleeves.

The drums and shrieking fifes played "God Save the King." Methinks the British were laughing. Crowds lined the streets to watch and cheer. For shame! Philadelphia is the land of Tories, they are everywhere. People I have seen at market, neighbors, Polly's parents . . . they clapped and yelled "Long Live King George." Polly stood by her father, but cheered not. Mayhap in her heart she is still a Patriot.

Following the Redcoats were baggage carts, cows, donkeys, goats, and many poorly dressed women. Methinks they cook and do laundry for the army. Some carried little children on their hips. Alas, my candle is a puddle of wax . . . cannot see . . . I shall write on the morrow.

Sunday, the 28th of September

This is how it happened that we are housing our enemy:

After the terrible parade we walked home. Whilst we were eating supper someone rapped on our door. 'Twas two Redcoats. Behind them in the street were more on horseback.

An officer named Major Quigley said he would stay with us. He asked us not! His men hammered a sign onto our post that says QUIGLEY'S HEADQUARTERS. Then they went to Miss Sarah's house. Her face turned pale when they knocked off her padlocks with the butts of their guns. They wrote with chalk on her door, AVAILABLE FOR OFFICERS' QUARTERS. There is no telling what damage those men shall do to her nice home.

We are distressed about another event. Today the Redcoats brought their wounded from the Brandywine battle on stretchers and in wagons. When they saw our hospital they made everyone get out of their sickbeds and go someplace else. Now our Patriots have no doctors to care for them. This I know . . . war is the cruelest thing.

Oh, to have Polly near me.

Two days later

I am burning with anger.

This morning I went to market for fresh beef bones. An English officer strolled by, a saber at his hip. He looked me up and down. "Pretty lass," he said, facing me. He grabbed my locket. I lifted my hand to stop him, but I was too late. He tore it from my neck. I wanted to slap him but thought better of it.

"Pray, tell me, is this thy father?" he asked upon looking at the picture inside.

My heart was in my throat.

The officer leaned close. His face was flushed in anger. I could smell the perfume from his wig. He whispered, "I know that your father is Thomas Nathaniel Potter, enemy of the king. Where is he now?"

I took in a breath, knowing not what to say.

"Answer me!" People in the market turned to look at us.

Such was my terror, tears came. I could not help myself. "I know not where he is, sir. 'Tis the truth. Please, may I have my locket back?"

He laughed, then looked again at Papa's portrait. "Sorry, lass," he said. "'Tis property of the king now." Still laughing, he put it into a pocket of his scarlet coat. As he walked across the street, I saw a bit of my blue ribbon hanging out at his waist.

I have cried until there are no more tears. What shall happen to Papa?

Evening, half past seven o'clock

A light rain has made the air feel cold. Mother said we must let Papa know 'tis not safe for him to visit us. The officer who took my locket now knows what he looks like. On the morrow I shall write a note. Since we know Papa serves under General Wayne, 'twill be easier to get a message to him. Ethan said his friend at the ship builder's will ride to that camp for three shillings. The friend said our army shall fight again soon.

I have the cat on my lap for warmth. She purrs as I pet her . . . oh, to be as calm as she.

Wednesday, the 1st of October

I pity the Patriots who fled the city. Their homes are being looted by the Redcoats. Major Quigley and his men brought in feather beds and blankets to put in our attic. They also carried in a chest of fine clothes that had been left behind by one of our Continental Congressman. Every time I walk along the streets I hear the sounds of parties and merry-making. Methinks our enemies rather enjoy this war right now.

Next day

Ethan came home from the ship builder's with a broadside — 'tis a piece of paper that had been nailed to a post. On it was a warning from King George:

REBELS HAVE UNTIL THE 25TH OF THIS MONTH TO TAKE AN OATH OF ALLEGIANCE TO HIS MAJESTY. IF YE DO NOT DO SO YE SHALL BE PLACED OUTSIDE OF ROYAL FAVOR.

Mother laughed, then threw it into the fire.

"Royal favor, fie! As for me and my house, we shall serve no king but King Jesus."

Methinks Mother is braver by the day. Seeing her so gives me strength.

Sunday, the 5th of October

A fearsome battle yesterday in Germantown. 'Twas so close we could smell gunpowder on the breeze. As there is no hospital for our wounded — and oh, so many Patriots have wounds — they have been taken to the Statehouse. There they lie on the cold floors, surrounded by their dying enemies. Our neighbors and other women hurried over there with rags and herbs to care for our men. In a panic I searched for Papa but did not see him, or Mr. Dean. I helped Mother bandage a man's leg that had been torn apart by cannonball. We fear he shall die without a surgeon. Our doctors are forced to treat the hated British before Americans. Thus many of our countrymen died before our eyes. We cared for them as tenderly as if for our own dear Papa.

I cannot sleep. Only in my prayers do I believe my father is still alive.

Wednesday, the 22nd of October

Rain.

Two weeks have passed since I last opened this journal, such has been my busyness. With soldiers in our home our cooking and laundry have doubled. Every night they play cards and sing. 'Tis one big party all through the city. Mother and I are weary beyond words. At night we fall into bed whilst whispering our prayers, then next thing we know the rooster crows . . . time to rise once again. Miss Sarah works with us yet her coming child makes her move slowly.

The first time I served Major Quigley I wanted to spit in his soup. My heart was cold, how I hated him. I carried his bowl to the table with a plate of warm bread. He smiled at me, then began to eat. I could see that his wig was crawling with fleas. There were sores on his cheeks from his scratching at them. His clothes had a foul vapor . . . methinks he has never washed.

At the sight of him I decided not to hate. He is just a flea-bitten man who is mine enemy. I do not have to enjoy his company, nor that of the other dirty ones with him. I do not want the Redcoats to set our house afire nor have cause to put us in gaol. Thus I shall be kind to them.

I forgot to say that Teacher came back to school. He has pox scars on his face the size of coins, but is most cheerful. I cannot attend, though, because Mother needs my help. I miss being able to see Polly.

Later, evening

'Tis half past eight. All are asleep save for the soldiers in front of our fire. They drink and laugh late into the night. I just read a proverb. 'Tis now my favorite, but I shall not stitch it to a sampler until the war is over:

If thine enemy be hungry, give him bread to eat; and if he be thirsty, give him water to drink: for thou shalt heap coals of fire upon his head, and the Lord shall reward thee.

I do not wish burning coals to befall mine enemies. But I do wish they return to England and that Papa come home to us. That shall be my reward.

Saturday, the 25th of October

This afternoon Major Quigley unrolled a scroll of paper onto our table. His officer took out a pot of ink and a quill for writing. He held up the pen for Mother.

"Ma'am?" he said. "Last day for signing the oath of allegiance to His Majesty."

My heart beat fast, such was my fear. If Mother refused they could drag us out of our home. I was glad my brother was at the harbor, else he may have done something rash.

Mother did not seem worried. She smiled at the soldiers, then bent over the fire. Carefully she ladled boiling water in our teapot.

I felt nervous watching her whilst the Redcoats waited. The silence in the room hurt my ears. Finally she set cups and saucers on the table and a plate of shortbread. Into their cups she poured steaming tea, then she wiped her hands on her apron.

"Sirs," she said, "ye may take me to gaol, but I shall sign no oath to King George."

The officer stood up. He looked angry and ready to grab his musket. I walked over to stand beside mother, to face the men. Miss Sarah did the same. I lifted Faith onto my hip. And thus we stood whilst the soldiers put on their tricorns.

"When this war is over," said Major Quigley, "accounts will be settled." Then he led his men out the door.

Before bed

When the Redcoats returned for supper they gave us no trouble. But their usual manners were gone. They did not look at us when we served them. Through the evening we had to hear their foul language and laughter. They told stories about cruelties toward Patriot prisoners. After Mother and I blow out our candle and before we sleep, we pray together. 'Tis easy to pray for Papa, and General Washington, and all the other soldiers. But 'tis hard to pray for the Redcoats.

Another day

No bell rang in the markets today, but I went anyway. There was no flour or meat to buy. No sugar or coffee. Supply ships are being unloaded for the armies, not for citizens. Our cellar is near empty. We have been feeding our own family plus six soldiers daily, sometimes more.

Thursday, the 30th of October

After breakfast Major Quigley bent down to pick up a shilling he had dropped. When he did so he flipped his wig! It slipped off his head to the floor. I dared not laugh, so I turned to stir the kettle. 'Twas the funniest thing I have seen in a long while. Of course I wrote Polly about it.

I have forgotten to say that our dressmaker has British officers quartered in her shoppe. When I take my letter, I curtsy to them. Though I keep mine eyes down I can see they are having a fine time with pastries and tall glasses of ale.

There are soldiers living in Miss Sarah's house as well, but methinks they are pigs. We hear crashing of furniture, then loud shouts. A boy delivering newspapers told us something terrible. He saw the men cut a hole in Miss

Sarah's parlor floor. There they squat to do their dirty business. Right over her well-stocked cellar. Now we know why we have not seen these soldiers out back using the privy. We are sick about this.

I am glad we did not leave the city, else the same would have happened to our home.

Friday, the 21st of November

Three weeks now without a quiet moment to myself. No time to write in this diary or even a note to Polly. She, too, is busy with soldiers in her home.

Next day

At seven o'clock this morning our house rattled. Bowls and spoons fell from the cupboard and one teacup broke. I cried out, thinking 'twas cannon fire nearby. But, nay, 'twas just an earthquake!

An hour later Ethan ran home from the harbor. He had climbed a ship's mast and could see smoke in the distance. He counted seventeen fires along the road to Germantown. The Redcoats are burning every barn and estate they can.

We are ready to flee to Valley Forge if they start burning Philadelphia. Mother and Miss Sarah have quietly packed baskets and hidden them in our room.

Sunday, the 30th of November

We did not go to church, but prayed at home and sang hymns. Such is our joy because we heard from Papa. He sent word through the ship builder. He shall not visit us until we let him know 'tis safe. Of course we kept this good news to ourselves. The officer who took my locket must never see Papa face-to-face.

The fires have stopped. Even so, we are ready to leave in the night if we must. The Redcoats' General Howe is letting citizens pass in and out of the city. But during daylight hours only. Now people are able to buy flour and meat from other areas.

Our spirits have been lifted as well by the sight of merchant ships in the harbor. General Howe has let them unload and set up shops along the docks. When I heard the bell ring I went to buy butter and brown sugar. To my joy I saw Polly! She, too, had a basket over her arm. 'Twas wonderful to see her. We spoke not, nor did we wave to one another. But her smile told me of our friendship.

I shall write her a letter about Major Quigley's fleas.

Before bed

A light snow is falling. The lamplighter came at four o'clock this afternoon, for the hours of sunlight are fewer. Soon the cold, dark months shall be upon us.

Friday, the 19th of December

After supper we heard Major Quigley talking to his officers. They said General Washington is taking his army to Valley Forge for the winter. 'Tis not fair that our soldiers must sleep in tents in the snow whilst the Redcoats have warm houses.

"But this is war," Mother said. "And nothing about war is fair."

Faith is asleep on the trundle, under our quilt. The lace on her nightcap frames her little face. Methinks she looks like a pretty doll. I pray she never sets eyes on a battle.

I go to bed tonight thankful. We have food and soft feather beds. Polly and I are still friends. Miss Sarah shall soon have a new baby and Papa is safe. Mother said mayhap we could visit him and Mr. Dean for Christmas. 'Tis just one week away!

Oh, Faith is stirring . . . I must blow out this candle. I think I will sleep well.

Historical Note

The year 1777 began with no one knowing how the war would end. Both the British and the American armies had the chance to win it. But neither did.

General George Washington won a big victory at Trenton on Christmas Eve of 1776. But there were terrible problems: His soldiers had no

winter clothes, and little food. Also, on January 1, enlistments for many of his troops would be up and they could go home to their families. Washington

Surrender at the Battle of Trenton.

pleaded with is men to reenlist. And they did.

Meanwhile, General Cornwallis was ordered to march his army of 7,000 men plus artillery through New Jersey. The plan was to trap Washington's soldiers against the Delaware River near Trenton and destroy him once and for all.

But on January 2, Washington's army slipped away in the middle of the night. They left burning campfires to trick the enemy into thinking they were asleep in their tents. The next day General Washington attacked British troops at Princeton and won another victory.

In August, General William Howe made his plans to capture Philadelphia. It was the capital and the largest city in the Colonies. Also, it was there that the Statehouse bell, later named the Liberty Bell,

The Statehouse in Philadelphia.

The Battle of Brandywine.

was rung after the Declaration of Independence was signed.

Eight months later the armies collided at Brandywine Creek, just outside Philadelphia. Two weeks later, on September 26, the victorious British soldiers entered the city where they spent the winter in citizens' houses. By this time, the Continental Congress had fled Philadelphia, and the Liberty Bell had been carried to safety, north to Allentown.

Carrying the Liberty Bell to safety.

Washington then took his army to Valley Forge. Though just seventeen miles away from their enemy, the Patriots camped through the cold winter in tents and crude log huts.

Winter camp at Valley Forge.

The war would rage for four more years before the British finally surrender.

About the Author

Kristiana Gregory had a lot of fun returning to the Philadelphia area to research *We Are Patriots*, a sequel to *Five Smooth Stones*. "I visited children at Valley Forge Elementary School and was excited that *they* were excited to read stories about their local history. It's a great adventure for an author to imagine what life might have been like for kids during Colonial America." Gregory loves writing on this subject because several of her ancestors served in General Washington's army. Her other story set in 1777 is *The Winter of Red Snow: The Revolutionary War Diary of Abigail Jane Stewart*, which was made into an *HBO Dear America* movie.

Also on HBO was Kristiana Gregory's *Royal Diary, Cleopatra VII: Daughter of the Nile*. Her other Dear America titles are *Across the Wide and Lonesome Prairie: The Oregon Trail Diary of Hattie Campbell*; *The Great Railroad Race: The Diary of Libby West*; and *Seeds of Hope: The Gold Rush Diary of Susanna Fairchild*.

Kristiana Gregory's first historical novel, *Jenny of the Tetons*, won the 1989 Golden Kite Award from the Society of Children's Book Writers. In 1993 *Earthquake at Dawn* won the California Book Award for Juvenile Literature for ages 11–16. *The Stowaway: A Tale of California Pirates* was voted a Best Children's Book of 1995 by *Parents' Magazine*. She lives with her husband and their two sons in Boise, Idaho.

Acknowledgments

Thank you to Thomas Tulba at Independence National Historical Park in Philadelphia, for his kind generosity in answering questions and directing me to source material.

Grateful acknowledgment is made for permission to reprint the following:

Page 102: Surrender at the Battle of Trenton, North Wind Picture Archives.

Page 103: The Statehouse in Philadelphia, North Wind Picture Archives.

Page 104 (top): The Battle of Brandywine, North Wind Picture Archives.

Page 104 (bottom): Carrying the Liberty Bell to Safety, Super Stock.

Page 105: Winter Camp at Valley Forge, North Wind Picture Archives.

Other books in the My America series

Corey's Underground Railroad Diaries
by Sharon Dennis Wyeth
Book One: Freedom's Wings
Book Two: Flying Free

Elizabeth's Jamestown Colony Diaries
by Patricia Hermes
Book One: Our Strange New Land
Book Two: The Starving Time

Hope's Revolutionary War Diaries
by Kristiana Gregory
Book One: Five Smooth Stones

Joshua's Oregon Trail Diaries
by Patricia Hermes
Book One: Westward to Home

Virginia's Civil War Diaries
by Mary Pope Osborne
Book One: My Brother's Keeper
Book Two: After the Rain

Dedicated to a new patriot, Han Shu-Chuan Gregory, with admiration and love.

Copyright © 2002 by Kristiana Gregory

Library of Congress Cataloging-in-Publication Data
Gregory, Kristiana
We are patriots / by Kristiana Gregory.
p. cm. — (My America)
Summary: In her diary, ten-year-old Hope writes about her life as a patriot in 1777 Philadelphia, as the Redcoats try to take over her city and defeat the Continental Army.

ISBN 0-439-21039-9; 0-439-36906-1 (pbk.)

1. Philadelphia (Pa.) — History — Revolution, 1775–1783 — Juvenile fiction.
[1. Phildelphia (Pa.) — History — Revolution, 1775–1783 — Fiction.
2. United States —History — Revolution, 1775–1783 — Fiction.   3. Diaries — Fiction.]
I. Title.   II. Series.

PZ7.G8619 We 2002
[Fic] — dc21   2001093847

10 9 8 7 6 5 4 3 2 1   02 03 04 05 06

The display type was set in Nicholas Cochin.
The text type was set in Goudy.
Photo research by Dwayne Howard
Book design by Elizabeth B. Parisi

Printed in the U.S.A.
First edition, May 2002